Just Perfect

written & illustrated by

Jane Marinsky

David R. Godine · Publisher

Boston

First published in 2012 by
David R. Godine · *Publisher*
Post Office Box 450
Jaffrey, New Hampshire 03452
www.godine.com

*Library of Congress
Cataloging-in-Publication Data*

Marinsky, Jane.
Just perfect / written and illustrated by Jane Marinsky.
p.   cm.
Summary: A child tells of seeking the perfect one to add
to a family of three, and after trying various pets
discovering that a baby is the perfect fit.
ISBN 978-1-56792-428-2
[1. Babies—Fiction. 2. Pets—Fiction. 3. Family life—
Fiction. 4. Brothers and sisters—Fiction.]
I. Title.
CURR PZ7.M33887Jus 2012
[E]—dc22
2010046262

First Edition
Printed in China

Dedicated to Leah, Rebecca, and Anna

Mommy, Daddy,
and I made three,
but we thought we
might like four.
So . . .

We got a dog,
but it shed too much.

Walking the turtle took forever.

The chameleon liked
to disappear.

The dolphin needed too much water.

The octopus made
a mess of everything!

The rooster woke up
way too early.

The porcupine
was hard to hug.

The owl was annoying,
always asking questions!

We looked high.

And we looked low.

But nothing fit just right.

Until, at long last,
you arrived.
And you were
just *perfect*.